9 5086 00368439 4

W9-BLP-717

For Rebecca Jane

—J.D.

Macmillan Publishing Company is part of the Maxwell Communication Group of Companies.

Macmillan Publishing Company
866 Third Avenue
New York, NY 10022

Originally published by Andersen Press, London, England.

First American edition

Printed in Italy by Grafiche AZ, Verona.

10 9 8 7 6 5 4 3 2 1

The text of this book is set in 16/19pt Times Roman
by Tek Art Ltd, Addiscombe, Croydon, Surrey, England.

The illustrations are rendered in watercolor.

Library of Congress Cataloging-in-Publication data is available.
ISBN 0-02-733195-4

LOLLOPY

written by JOYCE DUNBAR

illustrated by SUSAN VARLEY

MACMILLAN PUBLISHING COMPANY
New York
MAXWELL MACMILLAN INTERNATIONAL
New York Oxford Singapore Sydney

It was bluebell time in the woods. Sophie wasn't allowed to walk there alone so she took her toy rabbit with her. Sophie's toy rabbit had long, lollopy ears and long, lollopy arms and long, lollopy legs.

Sophie called him Lollopy.

"CAN you see the bluebells?" she said, lifting his big heavy head so that he could see. She was sure that Lollopy nodded.

Sophie wandered farther and farther into the woods, where the bluebells grew thicker and thicker. She stopped to pick a bunch of bluebells. As she picked more and more, Lollopy slipped from her hands.

WHEN Sophie got home her mother put the bluebells in some water.

"They're lovely," she said, "but you know you mustn't wander off into the woods by yourself."

"I didn't," said Sophie. "I took Lollopy, and - oh! I've lost him!" Sophie was nearly in tears.

"Don't worry," said her mother. "We'll look for him tomorrow."

THE moon came up in the sky. Lollopy's head hung down. When the rabbits tried to come out of their burrow, they found something in the way.

"It's the Bogey-Rabbit!" said Twitch.

"He's come to take us away!" said Tinker.

"He's going to eat us all up!" said Snuff.

"NONSENSE," said their mother and nudged her way past. Lollopy slumped over on his side. All the rabbits came out to look.

"What is it?" asked Snuff.

"Is it alive?" asked Twitch. Mother Rabbit lifted Lollopy's ears so that she could see into his eyes. Sophie understood his eyes. So did Mother Rabbit.

"He's Lollopy!" she said. "And he's lost."

"We'll look after him," said her children. "He can join in our games."

BUT when they tried to play hide-and-seek with him, Lollopy just lolloped in a heap. And when they played rough-and-tumble, he lolled about, any old way. Even when they teased him, Lollopy took no notice. They decided he was no fun at all!

"I know what would make him jump," said Tinker. The others looked at him, wide-eyed.

"Not the Bogey-Rabbit!" said Twitch.

"We wouldn't dare," whispered Snuff. But they knew they were going to try.

WHILE their mother was dozing, they carried Lollopy into the woods. Farther and farther they went, into the deepest, darkest middle, where the big bad Bogey-Rabbit lurked. There was silence and stillness all around.

"What does he look like?" asked Twitch.

"How will we know if it's him?" said Snuff. All of them shivered with fear.

"LOOK! The Bogey-Rabbit's ears!" whispered Snuff.
"Look! The Bogey-Rabbit's eyes!" murmured Twitch.
"Help! The Bogey-Rabbit's teeth!" yelped Tinker.
And the rabbits ran all the way home!

T

"WHERE have you *been*?" said their mother. "You know you mustn't wander off by yourselves."

"The Bogey-Rabbit got Lollopy!" they said.

"We didn't mean to!"

"We were only playing!"

"We just wanted to make him jump!"

THEY found Lollopy the next morning. He did look a sorry sight.

"It wasn't a Bogey-Rabbit that got him," said their mother. "But it might have been a fox and it might have got one of you instead. You're not so easy to mend."

She sewed Lollopy's ear back on and patched up his leg. Her children made him a dandelion medal on a bluebell chain, because they were sorry, and because he had been so brave. Then they left him, sitting by a tree.

IT was Sophie's mother who saw him first but it was Sophie who picked him up.

"Look at his ear and his leg!" she said.

"He's had an accident," said her mother. "But who could have patched him up?"

"And who made him a bluebell chain?" said Sophie, giving him a great big hug. And Sophie told Lollopy never to go into the woods again, not even if she went with him.

AND he never did.